SOME DAYS: *A Tale of Love, Ice Cream, and My Mom's Chronic Illness*
Copyright © 2021 by Julie A. Stamm
Illustrations copyright © 2021 by Chamisa Kellogg

The Experiment, LLC
220 East 23rd Street, Suite 600
New York, NY 10010-4658
theexperimentpublishing.com

THE EXPERIMENT and its colophon are registered trademarks of The Experiment, LLC. Many of the designations used by manufacturers and sellers to distinguish their products are claimed as trademarks. Where those designations appear in this book and The Experiment was aware of a trademark claim, the designations have been capitalized.

The Experiment's books are available at special discounts when purchased in bulk for premiums and sales promotions as well as for fund-raising or educational use. For details, contact us at info@theexperimentpublishing.com.

Library of Congress Cataloging-in-Publication Data available upon request

ISBN 978-1-61519-810-8
Ebook ISBN 978-1-61519-811-5

Jacket and text design by Beth Bugler
Author photographs by Amy Ciscool (Julie A. Stamm) and Christine Fuqua, Atomic Moose Photography
(Chamisa Kellogg)

Manufactured in China

First printing September 2021
10 9 8 7 6 5 4 3 2 1

Some Days

A Tale of
Love, Ice Cream, and
My Mom's Chronic Illness

Julie A. Stamm

Illustrated by Chamisa Kellogg

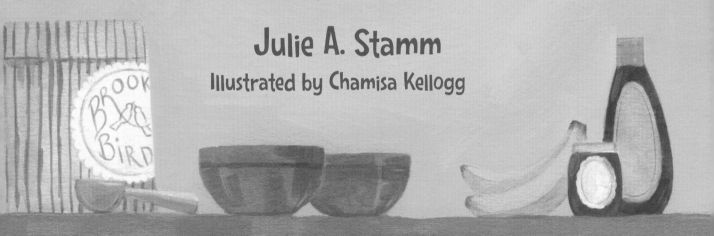

THE EXPERIMENT

NEW YORK

Everything is for Jack.

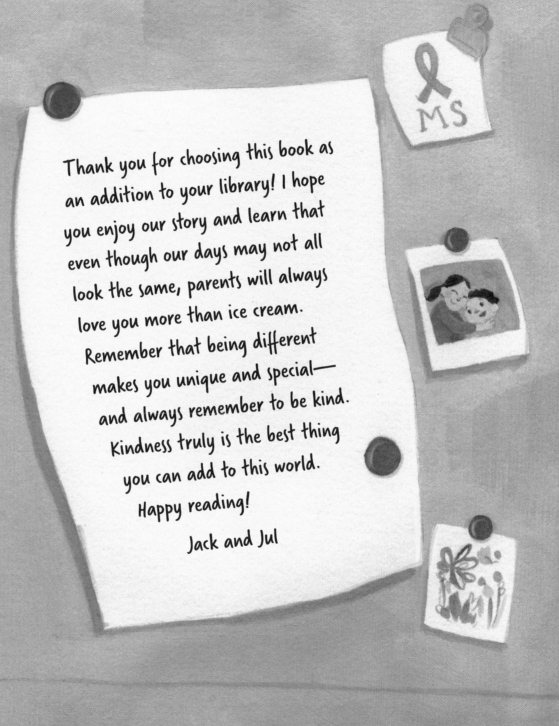

Thank you for choosing this book as an addition to your library! I hope you enjoy our story and learn that even though our days may not all look the same, parents will always love you more than ice cream. Remember that being different makes you unique and special— and always remember to be kind. Kindness truly is the best thing you can add to this world. Happy reading!

Jack and Jul

Hi! My name is Wyatt,
and this is my mom, Rosie.

My mom is super! But some days, she may not feel so super.

My mom has

mupi...

mulitap...

multiple scalos...

M.S.

Every day, she uses her
superpowers to battle her MS.

She says there are people all
over the world who have
chronic illnesses, just like her.

Our days are always filled with adventures!

Some adventures are **big** . . .

and some are small.

GATES A-C | BAGGAGE CLAIM

Some days, we have **REALLY** exciting plans, so Mom needs to save her energy.

I push her special chair and it's like Mom's very own roller-coaster ride.

SUPERHERO LAND

FUNN CAKE

Now she's ready for the real thing.
We made it—SUPERHERO LAND!

Some days, she's tired, so I bring my toys to her
and we play in our special fort just for two!

Sometimes, we just cuddle
on the sofa with my
favorite books or a movie.

Some days, her legs hurt,

and we can't go running around.

But she knows that I **LOVE** trains, so all aboard the mom train!

CHOO CHOOOO

We scooch all over the apartment.

Some days, Mom is a little wobbly . . .

so I get her magical stick,
and we cast spells
on my toys!

PEW!

PEW!

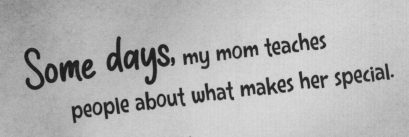

Some days, my mom teaches people about what makes her special.

Everyone thinks she is a superhero!

But **I know** her best superpower—
chocolate chip pancakes!

Some days, Mom takes forever to get ready.

Waiting is not easy, but
Mom has helped me practice.

Now it's Mom's
turn to wait!

Some days, it's too hot out for her.

Off we go on "Air Conditioner Missions,"
where we hop from shop to shop to keep cool!
(Sometimes, we even get ice cream.)

Some days, she needs to use the bathroom very quickly.
So we play fun games like "Spot the Potty!"

$1.99 /LB

3 for $1

The first person to find the restroom gets a prize.

RESTROOM

Some days, we head to the city for a big **FUNraiser!**

Everyone comes together to celebrate **MY** mom.

She says that all my hard work will lead to a cure
one day. I think that makes me a scientist!

Sometimes, Mom has to go to the hospital,
but not because she got hurt.

She just needs special medicine to help her stay strong.

When she gets home, I give her a huge hug and kiss. She says,

"That's the best medicine of all!"

She says no matter what we may face,

she will always love me more than anything in the world—
even **ICE CREAM!**

Each day is a new adventure,
filled with love . . . with my
favorite superhero!

The end

Julie A. Stamm was diagnosed with multiple sclerosis (MS) in 2007. Since then, Julie has made it her mission to educate, advocate for, and support others battling the disease, giving her the opportunity to work with physicians, patients, and foundations across the globe. She lives with her partner, son, and two pups in Colorado.

As a mother with MS, Julie searched for materials that could help her son understand her diagnosis—but found that nothing captured the positive, unapologetic message she wanted to portray. Instead, she wrote *Some Days*. The book reflects actual moments lived by Julie and her son, serving as a tool to reinvent the perception of chronic illness and empower the children battling alongside their superhero parents.

@imstamm

Chamisa Kellogg is an illustrator based in Portland, Oregon. She has made work for children's books, brands, games, and animation. Chamisa enjoys creating art that celebrates compassion, hope, and connection. In her free time, she bakes bread, wanders in the Oregon woods, and pokes around her garden.

chamisakellogg.com | @chamisafe